D0548776

Three Sensible Adventures

Stories by
Greg Wilson

Art by
William Lytle

Annick Press

Toronto • New York • Vancouver

Design by Sheryl Shapiro.

Annick Press Ltd.

We acknowledge the support of the Canada Council for the Arts for our publishing program. We also thank the Ontario Arts Council.

We acknowledge the financial support of the Government of Canada through the Book Publishing Industry Development Program for our publishing activities.

Cataloguing in Publication Data
Wilson, Greg, 1963-
Three sensible adventures

ISBN 1-55037-599-7 (bound) ISBN 1-55037-598-9 (pbk.)

I. Lytle, William. II. Title.

PS8595.I5833T47 1999 jC813'.54 C99-930680-4
PZ7.W6948Th 1999

The art in this book was rendered in watercolors.
The text was typeset in Veljovic.

Distributed in Canada by:
Firefly Books Ltd.
3680 Victoria Park Avenue
Willowdale, ON
M2H 3K1

Published in the U.S.A. by Annick Press (U.S.) Ltd.
Distributed in the U.S.A. by:
Firefly Books (U.S.) Inc.
P.O. Box 1338
Ellicott Station
Buffalo, NY 14205

Printed and bound in Canada by
Kromar Printing Ltd., Winnipeg, Manitoba.

Contents

The Puppet, the Troll, and the Hunter

Once upon a time there were two sisters, whose names were Red Tam and Green Tam.

Red Tam was the eldest, because the witch who made them made her first. She was stronger than anyone you've ever met. One day, just for fun, she picked up the hill behind her house and moved it out from under the road. The farmers who lived nearby were grateful, as their horses no longer had to pull their carts all the way up the hill. When winter came Red Tam put the hill back, so that children would have somewhere to toboggan.

Green Tam was as slender as her sister was strong. Her hair was as tangled as the wool in her knitting basket. All the animals loved Green Tam. One day, as she sat reading in the back yard, a squirrel climbed up her leg and fell asleep in her pocket. Green Tam sat without moving a muscle till the next morning, when Red Tam announced she'd made porridge with brown sugar and crunchy beetles for breakfast. There was nothing Green Tam liked more than porridge with brown sugar and crunchy beetles, so she put the sleeping squirrel in a tree and followed her sister inside.

One morning the sisters were baking bread when they heard a knock at the door. "Now, who could that be?" wondered Red Tam. "It's much too wet for visitors." When she opened the door she saw a little puppet, standing in the rain. The puppet was dressed in green, blue, yellow, and other colors so bright they didn't even have names.

"Help!" begged the puppet. "Please help me! Someone stole all my friends from the circus last night!"

"Why, that's terrible!" said Red Tam. "Come in and dry off before your hinges get rusty, and tell us what happened."

The puppet sat down (not too near the fire, because he was made of wood). Yesterday evening, he told them, after the circus went to bed, a thief crept out of the forest and into the wagon where the puppets were sleeping. The thief took the puppets from their shelves and stuffed them into a huge bag.

"I was the only one he missed," said the

puppet. “I always sleep on the very top shelf, so he didn’t see me.”

Just then the sisters heard another knock at the door. “Oh no!” said the puppet. “If anyone sees me, they’ll think I’m running away from the circus!”

“Quick!” said Red Tam. “Hide in our knitting basket!”

Green Tam opened the door to find the police constable from the village. “Good morning,” said the constable. “May I come in?”

“Who is it?” called Red Tam. Quickly she pushed the puppet into the basket, pulling the wool over his head.

“It’s the constable,” said Green Tam.

“Well, show her in,” said Red Tam. “Come warm yourself before the fire,” she said to the constable.

The constable sat down in the very seat the puppet had chosen. “There’s an important meeting tonight,” she told the sisters. “A hunter from the forest has terrible news about Erasmus the Troll.”

The sisters looked at one another. All the children in the village were frightened of

Erasmus, whose teeth were as long and yellow as bananas, but much, much sharper. Green Tam told the constable they would certainly come to the meeting, and gave her a loaf of bread warm from the oven. As soon as the door had closed the puppet sat up.

"Did you hear?" he squeaked. "She said a hunter from the forest! The thief who stole my friends came from the forest too!"

"Hmm," said Red Tam. "Something's not right about this. Something's not right about this at all."

That evening the witch's daughters walked to town. The meeting hall was full, but they found seats near the back. As the clock struck seven the door flew open, and a tall man strode up to the stage. He wore a broad-brimmed hat, and his long blonde beard was tucked into his belt.

"People!" he thundered. "Listen to me! I am Hairy Harry the Hunter, and I am here to warn you of terrible danger!"

People gasped. "T-t-terrible danger?" somebody asked.

"Terrible danger," repeated Hairy Harry. "Last night, as I was walking through the forest, I heard deep growling. I hid behind a tree, and what do you think I saw?"

He paused to look over the crowd. Mothers had wrapped their arms around their children, and fathers were biting down hard on their pipes.

"Erasmus!" shouted Hairy Harry. "Erasmus the Troll! As he lurched along he was growling to himself. 'Tomorrow,' I heard him say, 'tomorrow I'll eat every last one of them!'

"It can mean only one thing," said Hairy Harry. "Erasmus is planning to sneak into the village tonight, while you're asleep, AND GOBBLE YOU UP!"

Somebody shrieked, and one of the children started to cry. "But I have a plan," said Hairy Harry. "The biggest and strongest men in the village must come with me to the forest, while the rest of you hide. When Erasmus arrives, he'll think you've run away, and he'll head back to his lair. But we'll be waiting for him! We'll cut off his head so he can never bother anyone again!"

People cheered. "An excellent plan," they said to one another. Some of them thanked Hairy Harry. Others were already rushing home.

"But —" Green Tam started to say.

"Shhh," whispered Red Tam. "I know: Erasmus never eats anything but bark and leaves. But if you speak up now, Hairy Harry will guess that we're onto his tricks. We need to find Erasmus, fast, and warn him!"

"I'll ask the owl who lives in Farmer Spludge's barn," said Green Tam. "He'll know where Erasmus is." Off she ran, as quickly as her legs would carry her.

"And I'll figure out why Hairy Harry would steal the puppets from the circus," said Red Tam to herself. She crossed her eyes and thought as hard as she could.

A few minutes later, Green Tam came running back. "The owl says Erasmus lives under the bridge over the stream by the hill next to the lake where the dam used to be," she said breathlessly.

"Good," said Red Tam. "And I've figured out Hairy Harry's plan. If everyone hides in the woods tonight, there'll be no one left in the village. Hairy Harry can sneak back with the puppets and rob everyone!"

"But why would the puppets help him?"

Green Tam asked.

"Hairy Harry must have tricked them somehow," said Red Tam. "Puppet heads are made of wood, after all. Hurry! We have to warn Erasmus!"

The sisters ran so fast they almost flew. They ran across the field where Farmer Spludge grew her pumpkins, and over the hill where the children held rock-rolling contests in the summer. Finally they came to the old bridge. Many boards had fallen away, and long streamers of green moss hung from the handrails.

"Erasmus!" shouted Green Tam. "Erasmus the Troll! We know you're here! Will you come out and speak with us?"

A deep voice answered from under the bridge: "Who's there? Who wants to speak with me?" A thick arm reached up and grabbed the handrail as Erasmus pulled himself onto the bridge. He was even larger and uglier than the witch's daughters remembered.

"Oh, it's you," he grunted. "You're no good to eat. What do you want?"

"Now, Erasmus," said Green Tam, "You

don't fool us. We know you only eat bark and leaves. But Hairy Harry the Hunter told the people in our village that you're planning to gobble them up. They're coming here tonight to cut off your head!"

"Huh," said the troll. "Like to see them try. Just because I eat bark and leaves, that doesn't mean I'm a sissy. If anyone tries to make trouble for me, why, I'll — I'll —." With one hand Erasmus ripped the branch from a pine tree, and stuffed it into his mouth. "You shee?" he asked, chewing noisily. "Thash wha I'll do!"

"But aren't you afraid the villagers will be too strong for you?" asked Red Tam. "Why, I'm smaller than most of them, but I'm still stronger than you."

"What?" roared the troll. "You, stronger than me? Why, you're just a child!"

Red Tam didn't answer in words. Instead she grabbed the bridge with both hands and lifted it, Erasmus still clinging to the handrail, right up over her head.

"Whoa!" shouted Erasmus. "If everyone in the village is as strong as you, I'm in real trouble. I'd better hide!"

"Yes," said Red Tam, "You'd better." And the troll scurried into the woods.

"I'll stay here," Green Tam told her sister. "When the men arrive, I'll get the animals to scare them, so they won't ever bother Erasmus again. He may be a cranky old troll, but he has as much right to live here as anyone else. You go back to the village and stop Hairy Harry!" Red Tam nodded, and ran off.

Green Tam climbed into a tree to wait. She hooted softly in Owl, then barked in Fox. Silently the animals gathered round her.

The men arrived a few minutes later, carrying pitchforks and hammers. Hairy Harry's big axe was slung over his shoulder. "You hide here," he told the men. "I'll go back to wait for the troll. When I see him coming, I'll warn you. As soon as he gets here, you hit him with your hammers and stab him with your pitchforks! Once he's down, I'll cut off his head with my axe!"

Then Hairy Harry disappeared into the woods.

"Hmm," thought Green Tam, high in her

tree. "Red Tam was right: he's headed straight back to the village." She hooted to the owls once more, then barked at the foxes. Odd noises rustled in the dark around the hiding men.

"Now!" cried Green Tam. A dozen owls swooped down from nowhere and battered the men's heads with their wings. A dozen foxes nipped at their ankles. The men shouted in terror. One of them raised his hammer to strike a fox, but Green Tam reached down from her tree and snatched the hammer from his hands. "I am the dread troll Erasmus!" she growled in a deep voice. "Beware! Beware!"

Dropping their weapons, the men fled in fright.

Back in the village all was quiet. Red Tam sat waiting on the roof of the meeting hall. Several minutes passed, and then: "Aha!" whispered Red Tam, as the brightly dressed puppets came walking down the main street of the village.

"Oh, that awful hunter!" thought Red Tam, as the first puppet opened the door to the shoemaker's shop, went in, and came out a

moment later with her arms full of shoes and boots. A second puppet was opening the bakery door when Red Tam stood up and shouted, "Stop! Hairy Harry has lied to you! Oh please, stop!"

Surprised, the puppets all stopped and looked up at Red Tam. But then another voice shouted even louder.

"Don't listen to her! She wants to steal from the villagers!" It was Hairy Harry, standing beside the meeting hall with his axe over his shoulder.

"That's a lie!" shouted Red Tam. "You're the one who's stealing!"

"Then why did the villagers come with me?" Hairy Harry asked the puppets. "You saw them leave town with me, didn't you? Red Tam wants you to leave so she can rob them!"

Puppet heads were spinning in confusion. But then another voice was heard: "Wait, no, stop! Listen to Red Tam! She's

telling you the truth!" It was the little puppet who had asked the sisters for help. He ran through the street, waving his wooden arms. "The hunter tricked the villagers into leaving! You must believe the witch's daughter!"

"Why, you noisy little pipsqueak!" snarled Hairy Harry. "I'll turn you into toothpicks!" He grabbed his axe with both hands and swung it through the air. Thwack! The puppet's head flew from its shoulders!

The puppets dropped everything and ran in all directions. Still waving his axe, Hairy Harry looked up at Red Tam. "Come on down so I can chop off your head!" he growled.

"Why don't you come up here instead?" suggested Red Tam bravely.

"Or over here?" rumbled a deep voice. The hunter spun around, then shrieked. Erasmus the Troll was standing right behind him, grinning to show off his enormous teeth. He grabbed the hunter's axe and popped it in his mouth.

Gulp!

Erasmus licked his lips, then grinned. "I usually eat bark and leaves," he said. "But not always." Hairy Harry ran shrieking for the woods, with Erasmus close on his heels.

Red Tam climbed down from the roof. "I hope Erasmus doesn't get indigestion," she said to herself. "Hairy Harry is so very

hairy. But that poor puppet! Let's hope Green Tam can fix him." She carefully picked up the little puppet and his head, and hurried home.

Green Tam was waiting for her. "Oh dear!" she said. "What happened to our friend?"

"Hairy Harry cut off his head," said Red Tam. "Can you fix him?"

"I think so," said Green Tam. "If you'll pass me my spider-web glue, and my bone staples, I'll see what I can do." She put six strong staples in the puppet's neck, then painted over them with glue. A moment passed. The puppet blinked and sat up.

"Where am I?" he asked. "What happened?"

"Never mind that," said Red Tam, helping him to his feet. "You need to get back to the circus." Green Tam gave him some crunchy beetle cookies, and they sent him on his way.

"Well, that was certainly an adventure," said Red Tam with a yawn.

"Yes, it was," said Green Tam. "But now the moon is up, and it's time for bed." So the sisters brushed their teeth and washed their faces, and climbed into their beds.

"Goodnight," said Red Tam.

"Zzzz," said Green Tam, who was already asleep.

The Dragon and the Grandfather Clock

School was over for the summer. The days were so long and warm that Red Tam and Green Tam just couldn't get down to their chores.

"If we had an adventure first," said Red Tam to her sister, "we'd be in the right mood to work." Green Tam agreed. So they opened the door, and off they went.

Before very long they found themselves in a small village by the sea, where a wooden bench overlooked the harbor.

"Good morning," said Green Tam politely to the man polishing his peg leg at the end of the bench. He was bald, and wore a green parrot on his shoulder. A hundred different flags were sewn onto his coat.

"And good morning to you," replied the stranger, who rolled his R's as a cat purrs. "Couldn't ask for a finer one, could you?"

"No, sir," agreed Green Tam. "The boats are beautiful, too." The harbor was lively with boats: stately ships with huge sails, rowboats taking grandmothers to market.

"Aye," agreed the one-legged man, "but

none so beautiful as me Fiddlesticks." He took an old pipe from his mouth to point at a sleek red boat, rocking gently with the waves. The word "Fiddlesticks" was painted across her bow.

The one-legged man sighed. "She's me pride and joy," he said. "Only thing in the world more dear to me heart was me old grandfather clock. But it was stolen by Wretched the Dragon before you lasses was even hatched."

"That's terrible," said Red Tam. "Why would a dragon steal your clock? Dragons never need to get up in time for school," she pointed out. "And they don't need to know how long something's been in the oven, because they just roast their food with their breath."

"Aye, it's a puzzle," the old man agreed. "Maybe Wretched stole that clock because he guessed how much it meant to this old sailor. Peg Leg Peter, they call me." He shook hands with Green Tam, and then with her sister.

"Fiddlesticks and me," he told them, "we sailed from the warm beaches of Brazil all

the way to Canada, where it snows every day and the people ride around on polar bears. We traded emu feathers from Australia for bananas grown in Iceland, where they heat their greenhouses with the steam from volcanoes. But one day I heard that clock ticking away in a barber-shop in Amsterdam. It was like the beating of me own heart, it was. That clock told me home was the only place this sailor hadn't seen enough of. So I traded me treasure for the clock, and Fiddlesticks brought me straight back here."

He sighed. "But that very first night, as I lay in me bed, I heard the sound of great big claws scritching and scratching across the shingles of me roof. I was so frightened I pulled the covers over me head! Next night, the very same sounds. And the night after that, too. I could hear it breathing: 'whuffff... whuffff....' " He shuddered.

"Was it the dragon?" asked Red Tam.

"Yes," said Peg Leg Peter. "It was Wretched. One night I couldn't take it any longer, so I opened the window and shouted, 'If you're going to eat me, hurry up!' Next thing I knew, I was looking right in its eyes."

He shuddered again, and the sisters with him. They knew that you must never, ever look into a dragon's eyes, because they can hypnotize you to walk directly into its mouth.

"When I woke up, both the dragon and the clock were gone. They tell me that Wretched lives in a cave on Desolate Island, but I'm too old to steal back me clock."

"Oh, stuff," said Red Tam. "You're never too old for adventures. Why, our mother is three hundred and twenty nine, and she has adventures all the time!"

"She wouldn't think about it twice," agreed Green Tam. "We were actually hoping to have an adventure ourselves. If you'll lend us Fiddlesticks, we'll sail to the dragon's cave and fetch your clock for you."

Peg Leg Peter shook his head. "Could never do that," he said. "Fiddlesticks is me pride and joy."

But then the parrot whispered in his ear. "Eh?" said the sailor. The parrot whispered in his ear again, and Peg Leg Peter nodded. "Yes," he said softly, "You're right. I used to sail her through the

roughest storms, and I didn't worry about her then." He sat up straighter and banged his peg leg on the cobblestones. "All right!" he said. "It's a deal! I'll lend you Fiddlesticks if you'll bring back me clock!" He stuck out his hand for the sisters to shake once more.

"Now, let's see," said Red Tam. "We'll need food, and water, and crunchy beetles for Green Tam...." She wrote out a list, then tore it in two and gave one half to her sister. Off they ran in different directions.

An hour later they met on the dock, where Peg Leg Peter said he'd be coming with them. "One last adventure for an old salt!" he said. "Besides, I just wouldn't feel right, letting someone else sail her."

When the wind caught her sails, Fiddlesticks practically flew across the water. "No-one's ever come back from Desolate Island," Peg Leg Peter told them as they sailed. "But sailors say the dragon's cave is just a big hole in the side of a cliff."

They sailed all afternoon. When night came, Peg Leg Peter showed them how to hang their hammocks from hooks in the ceiling. They took turns sleeping, so that two sailors were always on deck.

In the morning they reached Desolate Island. Red Tam kept an eye out for the dragon's cave, and Green Tam watched the sky above them. Once or twice she thought she saw the dragon in the distance, but each time it was just a seagull, gliding over the water with its wings outstretched.

"Over there!" shouted Red Tam. A thin strip of rocky beach lay between the ocean and the cliff. The cave itself was a deep, dark hole, the size of a house. Huge scratches marked the rocks where the dragon had sharpened his claws.

"The water's very shallow here," said Peg Leg Peter as he brought Fiddlesticks closer to shore. "As soon as I drop anchor, you two rush in and steal that clock as quickly as you can. If the dragon comes back while we're here —"

"— we'll be his breakfast, lunch, and dinner," finished Green Tam. Splash! went the anchor. Splash! went the sisters into the ocean. The water was so cold that their toes were numb by the time they reached the shore.

They had taken only three steps toward the cave when they heard Peg Leg Peter shouting in alarm. The sisters turned and clutched one another. There, skimming over the waves with his wings outstretched and smoke puffing from his nostrils, came the dragon!

Faster than they could blink, he swooped down on Fiddlesticks and tore away her sail with his long, sharp claws. Then he landed on the beach, just ten yards from the sisters. As the dragon turned his head to look at them, they smelled the hot-metal smell of his breath.

"Remember, don't look into his eyes," Green Tam whispered to her sister. "He'll hypnotize you."

"Hrrrrmmmmm," breathed the dragon. "What have we here? Thieves? Thieves come to steal my treasure?"

"We're not thieves!" said Red Tam angrily. "We're —"

"Shh —" said Green Tam, who had already

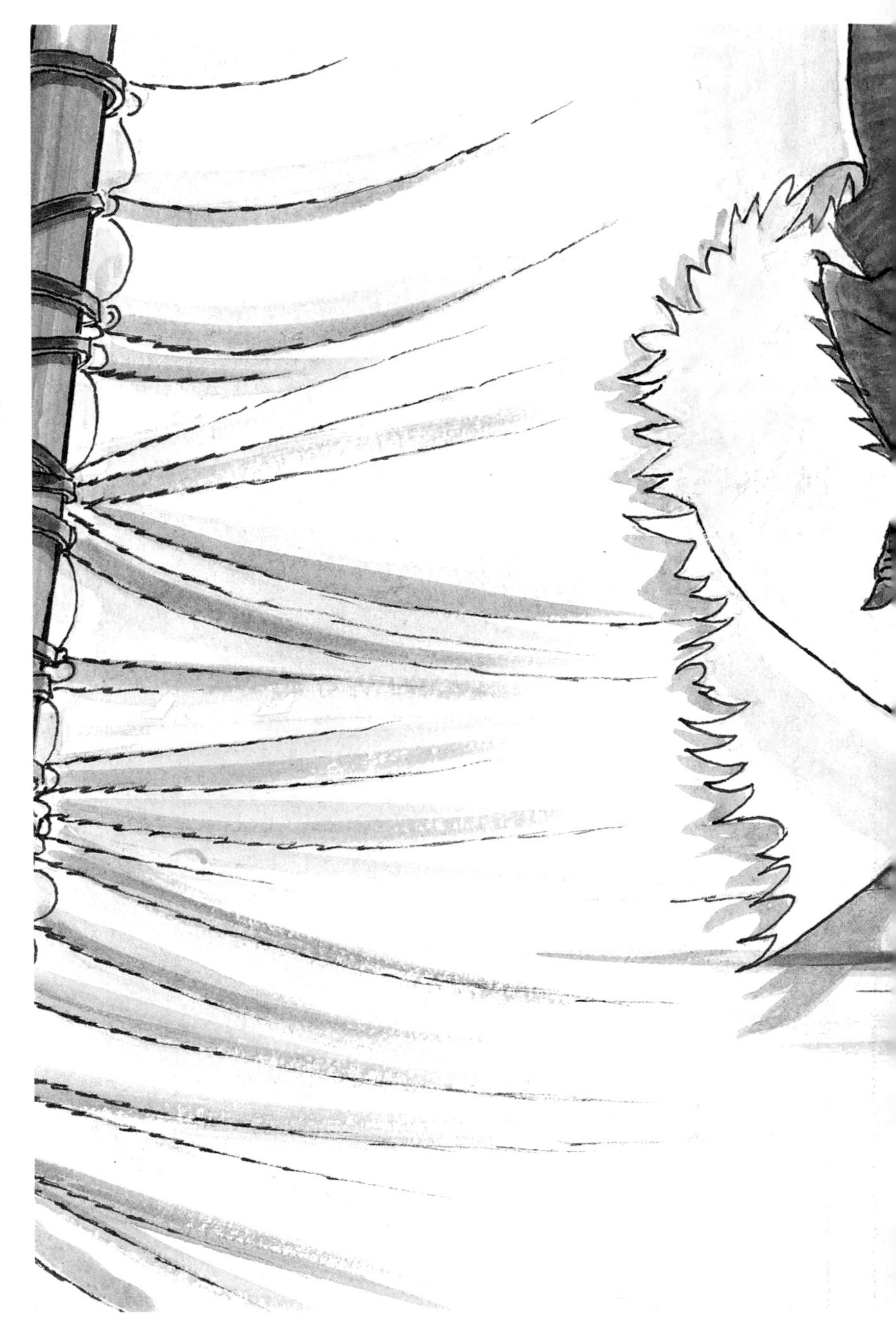

thought of a plan. "You shouldn't speak to strangers. We'll just wait for the dragon to come home."

"What?" roared Wretched. "I am the dragon! And I am going to eat you both for breakfast! RAAARRRRRRRRRR!!"

Red Tam put her hands over her ears when the dragon roared, but Green Tam only yawned. "Oh, don't be silly," she said when the noise stopped. "You're not a dragon. You're just a big iguana. We came here to see the dragon, because we'd heard that he was extremely handsome. We'll just wait until he gets home, if that's all right."

"What!?" roared Wretched. "Didn't you hear me? I said, I am the dragon!" Smoke poured from his nose, and his long tail whipped back and forth.

"Well, if you're a dragon, why aren't you breathing fire?" asked Green Tam.

"Fire, eh?" snarled Wretched. "Watch this!" He stretched out his neck and spat a great gush of fire onto a tree growing above the cliff.

"Hmmm," said Green Tam. "All right, so you can breathe fire. That still doesn't mean you are Wretched. Why, we've heard that Wretched is so smart, he even has a clock."

"What, that old thing?" said the dragon. "You just wait here." He hopped into his cave. "Ah, here it is!" He stuck his head back out of the cave with the grandfather clock in his jaws. "Nau oo oo bu'eve ah I' ah agon?"

"I beg your pardon?" said Green Tam sweetly. "I don't speak Iguana."

Wretched set the clock down. "Now do you believe that I'm Wretched?" he snarled.

"Maybe," said Green Tam. "But maybe not. Maybe Wretched moved to a bigger cave, and you're a new dragon who's taken over this cave."

This made the dragon even angrier. "Not Wretched!" he shouted. "Not Wretched! Of course I'm Wretched! Look at these teeth! Look at these wings! Who else would I be but Wretched?"

Green Tam shrugged. "If you really are Wretched, then tell us: where did this clock come from?" she added, crossing her arms.

"It came from a house in the town across

the water," said Wretched.

"And why did you take it?" asked Green Tam. "Only the real Wretched will know the answer."

"Why?" the dragon snarled. "I'll tell you why. Every time I flew over the village, I heard all the clocks going tick, tock, tick, tock, and families sitting down to eat their dinners, and parents telling stories to their children, and every night I thought, 'Everyone has a family except me. Everyone has a nice, warm bed except me.' So I decided to make my cave like a real home. I took the sails from a ship to make curtains, but my paws are too big to hold a needle and thread. I tore up the blackberry bushes to make a bed, but they dried out, and whenever I sneezed they caught fire. Finally, I decided I would get a clock to go tick, tock to me all night long. I went from house to house, night after night, listening to their clocks, until I found this one."

The dragon's head sagged. "But it was no good. It still goes tick, tock, but it doesn't

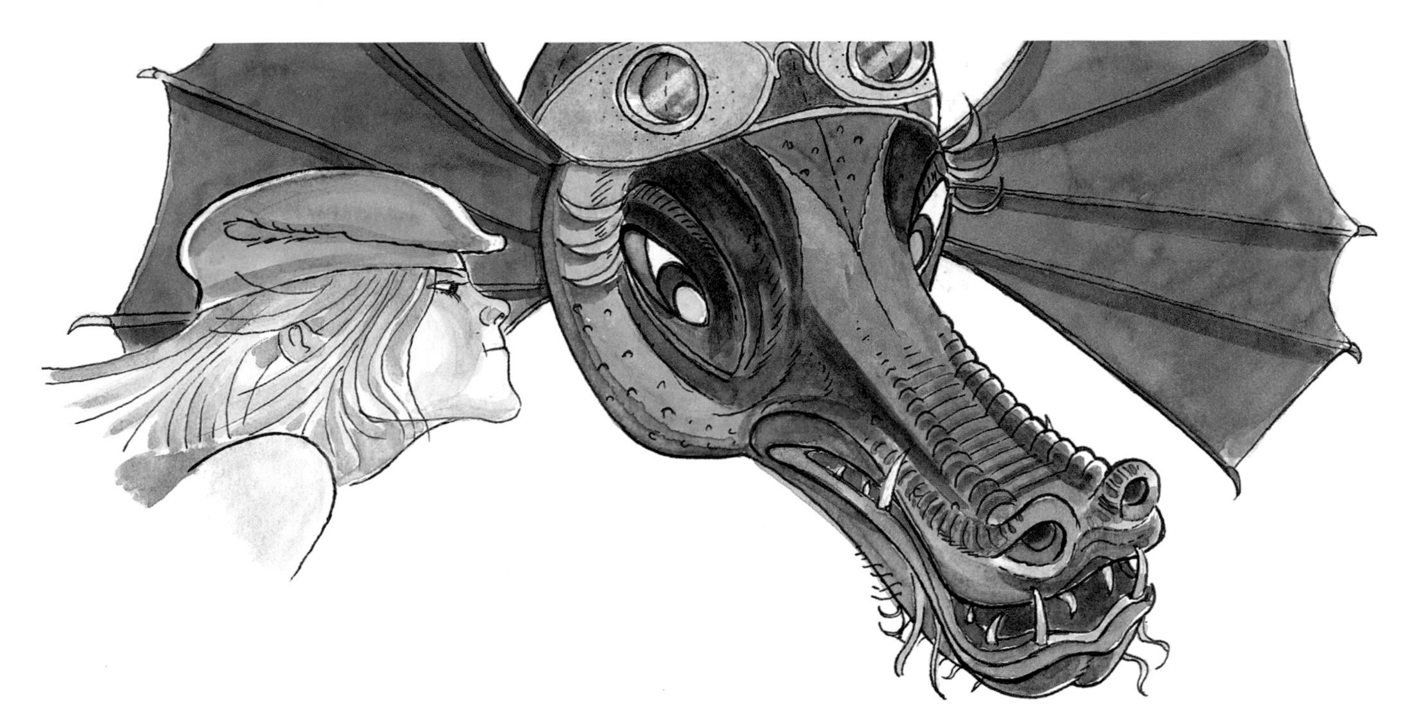

make my cave feel any more like a home. There must be some trick to winding it, but I've never figured it out." The dragon blinked, then narrowed his eyes. "Now, back to business. Which of you would like to be eaten first?"

"Not quite yet," said Green Tam. "You can certainly breathe fire, and you seem to know all about the clock. It's just — well, we'd heard that Wretched was a very handsome dragon."

The dragon swiveled his neck until his head was only inches away from Green Tam. "Are you saying that I'm ugly?"

"Oh, no, not ugly," said Green Tam quickly. "But when did you last look at yourself in a mirror?"

The dragon scowled. "What's a mirror?" he asked.

"It shows you what you look like," said Green Tam. "If you had a mirror, you could see for yourself whether you're handsome. There's one on our boat you could borrow if you want," she added.

"Hrrmmm," mused the dragon. "Is it like a painting? I've eaten paintings."

"Oh, it's much better than a painting," said Red Tam, having just figured out what Green Tam was doing. "Shall I get it for you?"

"No!" snapped the dragon. "I'll get it myself." He took ten quick steps through the water, holding up his wings to keep them dry (because the only thing a dragon hates more than getting its wings wet is rain going up its nose and putting out its fires).

"You there!" he roared at Peg Leg Peter. "Put down that parrot and bring me a mirror!" Peg Leg Peter pried the parrot off his arm, went into his cabin and returned with his shaving mirror. The dragon took it gently in his jaws, then bounded back to the beach.

"Here," he said, putting the mirror down in front of Green Tam. "Show me."

Green Tam picked it up and wiped it clean with her sleeve. "You have to look straight into it," she told the dragon as she held it up to his face. "Look straaaaiight into it —"

The dragon peered into the mirror.

"Ahhh," he breathed. "Is that me? Why,

I'm — I'm — ." His voice trailed off.

Green Tam waited a second, then another. Then she said softly, "Wretched? Can you hear me?"

"Yesss —" said the dragon slowly.

"He's hypnotized himself!" said Red Tam.

"Shh!" said her sister. "Wretched, why did you want your cave to be more like a home?"

"Because I'm lonely," the dragon replied slowly, staring at his reflection. "I have to sleep on cold, wet stones, with nothing but treasure and old bones for company."

"Haven't you ever had any friends?" Green Tam asked.

"When I was little," sighed the dragon. "We used to see who could breathe fire the longest, or fly the highest. But then I had to get a real dragon job, burning down villages and gobbling up people and stealing as much treasure as I could. I didn't have time for friends any more."

"But now you have all the treasure you need," said Green Tam. "I bet if you were to stop eating people, and stealing from them, you could have friends again. That would be

nice, wouldn't it?"

"Yesss —" said Wretched. "But then I wouldn't be much of a dragon, would I?"

"He's right," Red Tam whispered in Green Tam's ear. "Cats don't chase birds because they're bad, they chase birds because they're cats. It would be wrong to stop Wretched from breathing fire or stealing treasure."

"Oh, tush," said Green Tam crossly. "Let me think for a moment — I know! Wretched, I'm going to count to three. When I snap my fingers, you will wake up. You'll still be Wretched, but you'll only eat pirates, and you'll only burn pirate ships, and you'll only steal pirate treasure. Do you understand?"

"Only eat pirates," Wretched repeated slowly. "Yummy, smelly, pirates."

"Very good," said Green Tam. "Ready? One, two, three." She snapped her fingers.

The dragon blinked, then yawned. "Oh, it's you," he rumbled. "How nice to see you. Have you come to visit?"

"Yes, we have," said Green Tam. "That's what friends are for."

They spent the rest of the day playing on

the beach. Red Tam and the dragon lifted rocks to see who was strongest (they were about equal), and Green Tam and the dragon told each other jokes in Alligator and Crocodile (the dragon said Green Tam's accent was not bad, for a human). When Peg Leg Peter realized the dragon was no longer dangerous, he sailed over to join them.

The sun was setting when Red Tam patted the dragon on the head. "Well, we have to go now," she said, "but why don't you come to visit us? Peg Leg Peter could put you up."

"That's right," said the old sailor. "In fact, if you'd care to sleep in me old boat shed near the harbor, I'm sure the entire village would be pleased." (Peg Leg Peter knew he'd have some explaining to do, but he also

knew that his neighbors would be grateful for a live-in dragon to guard them from pirates.)

"Oh, that would be wonderful!" said Wretched. "But what shall I do with my treasure?"

Peg Leg Peter looked at the old gold and gems, and the bones in rusting armor, and shook his head. "Did it ever make you happy?" he asked.

"Not really," the dragon admitted.

"I doubt it would make anyone else happy either," said Peg Leg Peter. "How about we just leave it here – except for me clock, of course."

And so they stowed the grandfather clock on Fiddlesticks. With Wretched flying beautiful figure-eights above them, they raised their anchor and sailed for home.

The Prince and the Pirates

Red Tam and Green Tam stayed with Peg Leg Peter and the dragon for a week, sleeping in hammocks in the boat shed. One morning they woke to a tapping sound at their window.

Green Tam opened the window to find a weary seagull knocking the glass with its beak.

"Good morning," she said in Seagull. "You look like you've come a long way. Would you like some breakfast?"

"Thanks very much," said the seagull. "But don't I smell dragon? How safe is it around here?"

"Oh, that's just Wretched," explained Green Tam. "He's a good dragon."

"Hrmph," snorted the seagull. "No such thing as a good dragon! And I don't have time for breakfast, because I'm on a mission. I'm looking for someone brave."

"Well, your mission is over," said Green Tam. "Because that's us!"

"Phew," said the seagull. "I've flown day and night to find you. I'd be grateful if you'd read this note," it added, nudging the slip of paper rolled around its left leg. "My leg is somewhat itchy."

As Green Tam unrolled the note, Red

Tam came to look over her shoulder. "What's this?" she asked.

Green Tam cleared her throat. "To the Brave Person Who Reads This Note," she read aloud. "A dreadful pirate, Sneezy Simms, has kidnapped the Prince of Cats, and stranded me on this tiny island. Please come and rescue us!"

The witch's daughters had certainly heard of Sneezy Simms. He was the roughest, toughest, meanest pirate in the whole world! And his crew were even worse.

"This is dreadful!" said Green Tam. "Kidnapped! We have to do something!"

"Absolutely," agreed Red Tam, who was already stuffing a change of clothes into her pack. "We'll be on our way before you can say 'fibbedy fabbedy foo'."

Sure enough, the sisters were ready before the seagull had finished grooming its tail feathers. They found Peg Leg Peter in the kitchen, frying old tires for Wretched.

He shook his head when he saw the note, but wished them luck as they set off.

With the seagull flying overhead, the sisters hiked along the shore all afternoon. At night they slept with their packs under their heads. Around noon the next day the seagull swooped down suddenly, cawing "Hurry!" Directly across the bay was a tiny island, on which they could see a monkey in a bright green uniform tied to a stake. Orange and purple crabs were snapping at his toes.

"Hello, Mister Monkey! Do you need help?" shouted Red Tam.

"Oh, yes!" the monkey chattered. "Oh, yes please!"

"Why don't you get lunch ready while I rescue this monkey?" said Red Tam to her

sister, but Green Tam had already started to unpack the sandwiches.

Red Tam plunged into the water, swimming so quickly that she made a wake like a boat. When she reached the island she yanked the stake out of the ground with the monkey still tied to it, then swam back to shore.

"You're safe now," said a soggy Red Tam, as she untied the monkey. "But tell us who tied you to this stake?"

"Have some lunch first," said Green Tam, handing the monkey a sandwich (without crunchy beetles, because she knew some people didn't like them).

"Oh thank you!" said the wet monkey, dripping and eating at the same time. "But look at my poor uniform! If my master was here, I would be so ashamed."

Then he sat down on the sand and began his story. "It all started when my master had an argument with his father, the king. I don't know why they were arguing, but when the prince came to fetch me, his tail was twitching, and his whiskers went flick-a-flick. So I said, 'It's a beautiful day, Master. The wind is blowing. Why don't we sail across the ocean to see the other side?' We sailed for hours, past dolphins playing tag with turtles, and pink fish using their back fins as sails. We even saw a sea monster, but it was just a little one."

"How little is a little sea monster?" asked Red Tam.

"Oh, it only had one tree growing on its back, and would have had to stretch its jaws very wide indeed to swallow our ship," said the monkey. "We thought we'd be safe if we sailed behind it, because it wouldn't be able to see us. But the pirates had thought of that too, and were hiding behind the sea monster. They pounced on us, and their swords went snick-snack! They yelled rude things at my master as they fought. He cut the pants off three pirates, but they threw a net over him and tied him up tight. I tried to help him," the monkey said, sniffling again. "But I'm just a monkey. One pirate tripped me, and another tied me up, and then they rowed to this beach and left me for the crabs to eat!"

"Well!" said Red Tam. "When we find them, we'll cut off their pants and write rude words on their cheeks with crayons!"

"How?" asked Green Tam. "We don't know any rude words."

"Well, we'll invent some!" said Red Tam.

"But there are dozens of pirates," pointed out the monkey, "and only two of you."

"Well then," said Green Tam. "We'll have

them outnumbered!"

As soon as the monkey had finished his sandwich, they set off to find the pirate ship. Red Tam walked ahead so she could lift big rocks and logs out of their path. Every ten steps, she asked the monkey another question about the pirates. By evening, that poor monkey's jaw was almost as weary as his knees.

Then Green Tam found an abandoned rowboat, upside down on the beach. This gave everyone somewhere to sit while she made a fire and cooked hot dogs. Red Tam told a story about Grandmother Goblin and her silver shoes. The seagull told a story about two sisters who set out one day to rescue the Prince of Cats. "I don't know how it ends yet," said the seagull. "But I'm sure it will be exciting." And then everyone curled up and closed their eyes.

Suddenly it was bright morning. The waves were lapping at their feet. "Wake up, wake up!" cried the seagull, circling anxiously overhead. "Sneezy Simms is anchored just around the point!"

The Tams looked at each other. Now that

they'd found Sneezy Simms, what could they do?

"We could drop a great big net over the boat," suggested the monkey. "A really, really big net."

"But how would we drop it from above?" asked Red Tam. "I think we should challenge them to a heavy lifting contest."

"But they're pirates," said the seagull. "They might cheat. I think we should all fly into the air and drop rocks on their heads until they let the Prince go."

"But some of us can't fly," Green Tam pointed out. "I think we should sneak onto the pirate ship, rescue the Prince, and then row away as fast as we can." The others agreed that this was probably the most sensible thing to do (although Red Tam wondered whether you were allowed to be sensible when you were having an adventure).

They all climbed into the rowboat, and Red Tam rowed them quietly around the point. "There it is!" whispered the monkey. The pirate ship was painted entirely black, with a large skull and crossbones on her

mainsail. The seagull circled the ship, then came back to hover above them. "Can't see a lookout," it reported. "But I can hear lots of noise from down below."

Red Tam began to row even more gently, making hardly any sound. As they drew closer to the ship, they could hear rude songs from below deck, and the sounds of fierce arguments.

Red Tam brought the rowboat close to the anchor chain. "You first," she whispered to the monkey. "If anyone sees you, just jump — I'll catch you." The monkey scampered up the chain.

A moment later he was back. "No-one on deck," he whispered. "But the Prince's sailboat is still tied up on the other side!"

The monkey climbed the anchor chain again. Green Tam followed him, with Red Tam swift on her heels. Once on deck, they hid behind a cannon. The deck was empty, but loud singing could be heard beneath their feet.

"I'll untie the ropes to the Prince's sail-boat," said the monkey.

"I'll look up front," said Green Tam.

"I'll look at the back," said Red Tam.

"And I'll watch for pirates," said the sea-gull, flapping above them.

Red Tam crept to the stern of the ship: no prince anywhere. Suddenly the seagull swooped down and squawked in her ear: "Quick! Your sister's found the Prince, but the pirates are coming on deck!" Red Tam ran to the bow of the ship. There, tied to the mast, stood the Prince of Cats!

Green Tam was undoing the last of many knots. "There you go, Your Majesty," she said.

"Thank you," meowed the Prince. He had a deep meow, almost like a tiger's. "Thank you both. But my poor servant! I don't suppose you've seen a monkey in a green uniform anywhere, have you?"

"He sent us a note asking for help," Green Tam explained, "and right now he's untying your ship. We must hurry, or we'll never escape."

"ARRRR!!" roared a wicked voice close behind them, and the Tams jumped into the air. "Don't ye worry about escaping, lass! Ye'll never escape, no, not ever! ARRRR!" There,

standing behind them, were Sneezy Simms and his crew! And they all had swords in their hands!

The pirate captain had an evil snarl. "So, ye thought ye'd sneak up on me, did ye? Ah, but we saw ye coming, 'cause a pirate has eyes in the back of his head. Ye can't sneak up on Sneezy Simms, can ye, lads?"

"Never, captain!" shouted his pirate crew.

"And why not?!" shouted the captain.

"Because we're so clever!" shouted his crew.

"Huh," said Green Tam, thinking quickly, "if you're really so clever, how come you can't even tie up your own shoelaces?"

Every single pirate looked down at his shoes.

"Run!" shouted Green Tam. The Prince, Red Tam, and Green Tam sprinted for the side of the ship.

"After them! After them, you drippy-nosed clam-heads!" shouted Sneezy Simms. "And when ye catch 'em, ar, turn 'em into sausages!"

"Over here!" waved the monkey. The Prince leapt over the side and slid down the sail to the deck of his boat. Red Tam jumped and slid down behind him. Green Tam took a deep breath and —

"Gotcha!" sneered a cruel voice, as Green Tam found herself struggling in the mesh of a huge fishing net. An ugly pirate face leered above her. Green Tam had been captured!

"Go! Go!" she shouted to her sister and her friends. The monkey had already pushed the sailboat away from the pirate ship.

"Wait!" shouted Red Tam. "We can't leave her!"

"Bring help!" Green Tam shouted. The seagull flapped around her, then hurtled away into the night.

Behind her, pirate boots were heavy on the deck. Green Tam turned to face a grinning Sneezy Simms.

"Well, what a strange fish we've caught tonight," he said. "Come on, lads, tie her up. It'll be sausages for breakfast!" The crew laughed loudly, but through their laughter Green Tam could hear her sister's voice, far off, calling her name.

The pirates tied her up to the very mast from which she'd rescued the Prince of Cats. They left as a guard the ugly pirate who had

dropped the net on her. He sat beside her eating porridge and mussels, and whistling pirate tunes. Every once in a while a lump of porridge sprayed out of his mouth as he whistled, but he didn't seem to care.

"You'll be sausages in the marnin'," he told Green Tam.

"Oh, I don't mind," she said bravely. "Sausages can be very nice, if you put enough crunchy beetles on them."

It was a very long night. As Green Tam discovered, it's almost impossible to sleep standing up. Once or twice she thought she heard a bird flying overhead, but when she whispered, "Seagull?" no-one answered.

And then it was morning. The pirates woke slowly, grumbling about the bad taste in their mouths (pirates never, ever brush their teeth). Sneezy Simms emerged from his cabin and yawned a huge, evil yawn.

"ARRRR, look at this mess," he groaned. "I'll tell ye, girl, if ye'd do the dishes, I might let ye live."

"I'll only do them if you say 'please'," said Green Tam firmly, looking him in the eye.

Sneezy Simms scowled.

"Right, then," he snarled. "Somebody wake up the cook! Somebody get the oven started! It's sausage time!"

The crew began to cheer, but they were interrupted by the shouts of the pirate guard. "Captain! Look! They're coming back!" The pirates rushed over to the rail. Sure enough, far in the distance they could see the brave white sail of the Prince of Cats' boat.

"Har har har!" laughed Sneezy Simms. "Come back to rescue her, eh? Right, lads, load up the cannons! Let's give 'em a proper pirate hello!"

The crew rushed back and forth, pulling the lids off barrels of gunpowder, swabbing out the cannons with long-handled mops. In less than a minute, the cannons were loaded and ready to fire.

"Captain!" shouted the pirate in the crow's nest. "They're flying the white flag! They want to talk!"

"Grrr," grumbled Sneezy Simms. "I know it's a trick, but even pirates have rules. Very well!" he shouted. "Run up a white flag!"

A few minutes later, the Prince's sailboat pulled up beside them. Every cannon was pointed straight at the little boat. The Prince bowed. "Good morning, Mr. Simms," he said. "I hope you slept well."

"Better than yer friend," the pirate captain said. "The cook's got the stove goin' — will ye be wantin' to join us fer sausages?"

"Oh, I don't think so," said the Prince coolly. "There won't be time for sausages after you've surrendered."

The pirate captain blinked, then laughed loudly. "Surrendered? Surrendered!? Did ye hear that, lads? We're going to surrender!" The other pirates laughed loudly (one so hard that he got hiccups).

Sneezy Simms turned back to the Prince. "Now, why, might I ask, would me fine pirate crew want to surrender?"

"Because if you don't," said Red Tam from behind him, "our friend here will be eating a very big breakfast this morning."

The pirates whirled around. Sneezy Simms turned green, while the others screamed in horror. There, on the other side of their ship, was Red Tam, sitting on — sitting on —

"Hello," said Wretched. "In case you haven't noticed, I'm a dragon." He smiled so they could see his magnificent dragon teeth. "A dragon who only eats pirates."

It took but a second for Sneezy Simms to surrender, and only a few seconds more for Red Tam to untie her sister. As she unpicked the knots, Red Tam explained that the worried Wretched had spent yesterday flying along the coast in search of the sisters. He met the seagull, who led him to the sailboat and introduced him to the Prince of Cats. Together the friends had worked out their plan: the Prince of Cats would distract the pirates while Wretched and Red Tam snuck up behind them.

"I'm sure your father will be glad to see you," said Green Tam to the Prince. "Especially when you bring him these pirates as a present. Wretched will go with you to make sure they behave."

"Thank you," said the Prince to Wretched. "You are a very good friend indeed."

(The delighted Wretched puffed little smoke rings out of his nose.)

"And you are good friends as well," said the Prince to the sisters. "I'd be grateful if you'd take my little sailboat as a present." Then he shook hands with Red Tam and Green Tam. The monkey cheered wildly as the sisters boarded the sailboat, raised their anchor, and set sail.

And so the witch's daughters came back to the village. "Why don't you keep your new ship here, with Fiddlesticks?" suggested Peg Leg Peter. "Then it'll be ready for your next adventure."

The villagers were already missing the dragon. "Oh, he was marvelous for cleaning out chimneys," said one woman. "Just stuck his head in through the window, and fwoosh! Cleaned it right out."

"Don't worry," said Green Tam. "He'll be back before you know it." And after shaking hands with Peg Leg Peter one more time, the witch's daughters set off for home.